nickelodeon

DORA the EXPLORER

At the Carnival

Turn the page to learn with me and my very best buddy, Zee!

adapted by Leslie Valdes
based on the screenplay "The Big Piñata"
written by Leslie Valdes
illustrated by Robert Roper

Based on the TV series Dora the Explorer™ as seen on Nick Jr.™

SIMON SPOTLIGHT/NICKELODEON
An imprint of Simon & Schuster Children's Publishing Division
New York London Toronto Sydney New Delhi
1230 Avenue of the Americas, New York, New York 10020

For information about special discounts for bulk purchases, please contact Simon & Schuster Special Sales at 1-866-506-1949 or business@simonandschuster.com.
Manufactured in the United States of America 0112 LAK This Simon Spotlight edition 2012 2 4 6 8 10 9 7 5 3 1 ISBN 978-1-4424-3537-7
This book was previously published, with slightly different text.

In this book, you will learn to . . .

✓ **READ with us**

MOVE with us

SHARE and CARE with us

DISCOVER with us

CREATE with us

✓ **EXPLORE with us**

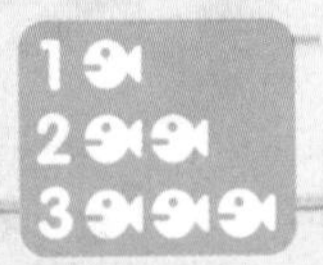

COUNT with us

MAKE MUSIC with us

Hey there! I'm Moose and this is Zee. We're so glad you picked up this book today. We have a feeling you're going to love what happens in this story!

A carnival is a wonderful place
for playing great games and painting your face.
Dora and Boots want to win the big prize
by collecting eight tickets for riding the rides.
Where's the Big Piñata? Just follow their trail—
and help Dora and Boots in this exciting tale!

Check out the last page for tips on making your very own piñata!

One day Dora and Boots were exploring the carnival. It was a fantastic place, full of colorful rides, great games, and sweet treats to eat! "I love carnivals!" Dora said happily.

"So do I," agreed Boots. "I can't wait to ride the rides, play the games, and try to win prizes."

Dora and Boots were going to try to win the greatest prize of all—the Big Piñata!

"When a piñata breaks open, all kinds of prizes fall out—like toys and treats," said Dora.

"And stickers, too," added Boots.

“To win the Big Piñata, we need to collect eight yellow tickets,” said Dora.

"How do we find the Big Piñata, Dora?" Boots asked.

"Who do we asked for help when we don't know which way to go?" Dora reminded him.

"Map!" answered Boots.

"*¡Sí!* Map can tell us how to get to the Big Piñata!" said Dora. "Say 'Map'!"

Map popped out of Backpack.

"Hurry, hurry, hurry!" he called. "To get to the Big Piñata, you have to go past the Ferris Wheel, and then go around the Merry-Go-Round. Along the way, you'll need to earn eight yellow tickets!"

"Thanks, Map!" said Boots.

"To the Ferris Wheel!" shouted Dora. "*¡Vámonos!* Let's go!"

At the Ferris Wheel, Dora and Boots saw their friend, Señor Tucán. Señor Tucán told them they could earn four yellow tickets by riding the Ferris Wheel.

"Let's go for a ride!" exclaimed Boots.

"We just need to find an empty seat," said Dora. "Our empty seat is marked with a star! Do you see a star?"

"There it is!" answered Boots. They ran over to take their seat on the Ferris Wheel.

Dora and Boots went up, up, and up! Soon they were way up in the air, high above the carnival.

"Whee!" squealed Boots.

"We can see the whole carnival from up here," said Dora. "Do you see the Merry-Go-Round?"

"Yes, I see it, Dora!" said Boots, pointing to the ground below.

When their ride was over, Señor Tucán gave Dora and Boots four yellow tickets for riding the Ferris Wheel. Yippee!

"Now we can go to the Merry-Go-Round!" shouted Dora.

At the Merry-Go-Round, Dora and Boots saw their friend Isa the iguana.

"Isa says that we can win more yellow tickets if we grab the orange ring," Dora explained.

"Let's ride the Merry-Go-Round and get that ring!" cheered Boots.

Dora and Boots each picked a colorful horse to ride on the Merry-Go-Round. It wasn't long before Boots pointed out the orange ring.

"Smart looking, Boots!" Dora cheered.

When their ride was over, Isa gave Dora and Boots four yellow tickets for riding the Merry-Go-Round. Yeah!

"Four yellow tickets for riding the Merry-Go-Round and four yellow tickets for riding the Ferris Wheel," said Dora. "So how many tickets do we have all together?"

Dora and Boots thought. "Four plus four equals . . ."

Dora quickly figured it out. "Eight! *¡Ocho!* We have eight tickets!"

"Now we have enough to win the Big Piñata!" Boots cheered.

Dora and Boots ran toward the Big Piñata. Suddenly they heard a familiar sound.

"That sounds like Swiper the fox!" cried Boots. "That sneaky fox will try to swipe our tickets."

"To stop him, we have to say 'Swiper, no swiping'!" said Dora. "Swiper, no swiping!"

"Oh Mannn!" Swiper said as he crept off.

Finally, Dora and Boots made it to the Big Piñata!

"Step right up!" announced the Fiesta Trio. "You need eight tickets to win the Big Piñata."

Dora and Boots counted their tickets for the Fiesta Trio—one, two, three, four, five, six, seven, eight! They had enough for the Big Piñata! *¡Fantástico!*

"Look!" exclaimed Boots. "All our friends are here to help us open the Big Piñata."

"To open the Big Piñata we need to pull the green ribbon," said Dora.

"I see it," said Boots.

"Reach out and grab it," Dora encouraged. "Pull!"

Hooray! Dora and Boots opened the Big Piñata. Toys and stickers and treats streamed down everywhere. It was the perfect end to a perfect day at the carnival!

"We did it!" Dora and Boots said together.

Dear parents,

We hope your child enjoyed this exciting Dora story. To extend this story, have a conversation with your child about it. You can ask him about his favorite carnival ride or have him tell you all about a time when he won a prize.

This book is also a great starting point for talking to your child about the diverse cultures that make up our world. In this story Dora and Boots's prize for collecting eight tickets is a special piñata. Piñatas are popular at parties and festivals here in the United States as well as in many Spanish-speaking countries. Your child can make his very own piñata by following this easy activity.

Simply Perfect Piñata

From your friends at Nickelodeon and Simon Spotlight

What you will need:

•An adult's help •Paper grocery bag •Markers, crayons, or stickers •Safety scissors •Tape •10 to 20 colored strips of construction paper or ribbon •Candy or little treats •Tissue paper or newspaper •Yarn or string

1. Decorate a paper grocery bag any way you like with markers, crayons, or stickers.
2. Have a grown-up cut a slit across the bottom of the grocery bag, leaving approximately a half inch on each side.
3. Tape long strips of colored construction paper or ribbon to the inside of the slit, and then tape the slit back up securely on the outside.
4. Fill the bag up about half way with candy or little treats. Fill the rest of the bag until it is nearly full with tissue paper or newspaper. Mix everything together, and then fold the opening of the bag down and tape it closed.
5. Hang your piñata from the ceiling or a tree branch with yarn or string and invite your parents or friends to take turns pulling ribbons until the bag breaks and the treats pour out.